Rebecca 2010 Dec 20

Books by Geri Halliwell

Ugenia Lavender

Coming Soon

Ugenia Lavender and the Terrible Tiger
Ugenia Lavender and the Burning Pants
Ugenia Lavender: Home Alone
Ugenia Lavender and the Temple of Gloom
Ugenia Lavender: The One and Only

Geri Halliwell

Illustrated by Rian Hughes

MACMILLAN CHILDREN'S BOOKS

*This is a work of fiction. These stories, characters, places and events
are all completely made-up, imaginary and absolutely not true.*

Ugenia Lavender X

First published 2008 by Macmillan Children's Books
a division of Macmillan Publishers Limited
20 New Wharf Road, London N1 9RR
Basingstoke and Oxford
Associated companies throughout the world
www.panmacmillan.com

ISBN 978-0-230-70140-3

Text and illustrations copyright © Geri Halliwell 2008
Illustrations by Rian Hughes
Brain Squeezers by Amanda Li

The right of Geri Halliwell to be identified as the
author of this work has been asserted by her in accordance with the
Copyright, Designs and Patents Act 1988.

1 3 5 7 9 8 6 4 2

A CIP catalogue record for this book is available from
the British Library.

Printed and bound in Great Britain by MPG Books Ltd, Bodmin, Cornwall

Contents

To Bluebell. Little girl, big imagination.

1

uGenia Lavender

The New Girl

It was early Saturday morning. The sun was climbing high as it blazed down on the golden sands of the desert. A short shadow began to creep from behind the gigantic pyramid where the stone met the sky. The wind whistled and blew a blanket of sand over the monumental masterpiece.

'Injustice! I don't want to leave here!' huffed Ugenia, looking around at the marketplace buzzing with people.

She rubbed her eyes and peered through the back of the dusty jeep window, taking her final glance at the gleaming pyramid as she said her goodbyes. Ugenia was leaving Egypt for good. She had spent many months there with her parents – Professor Edward Lavender, a dinosaur consultant and specialist in pretty much everything, and her mother, Pandora Lavender, who was a TV presenter and had been working on a holiday show. Ugenia's dad had been working on an archaeological dig. In fact, he'd been working on archaeological digs for as long as Ugenia could remember. The Lavenders had actually been travelling around the world for the last eight years, which was most of Ugenia's life. But now everything was about to change . . .

Pandora was starting a new job on *Breakfast TV* and Professor Lavender was going to work at a dinosaur museum in a small town called Boxmore . . . and all because Ugenia's parents thought it was time that Ugenia lived in one place and went to a proper school.

'Injustice! I really don't want to leave here, Mum. I mean, who's going to teach me now?' said Ugenia, who'd been quite happy having her parents as her teachers.

'You'll have real teachers, Ugenia,' Pandora said, smiling.

'Double injustice!' huffed Ugenia, feeling very grumpy, squashed amongst the trunks and cases. The jeep, which was stacked high with the Lavenders' luggage, rumbled along the jagged road, leaving Egypt behind in a dusty trail of memories.

Ugenia hugged her luminous yellow rucksack, which had all her important things in it – a bottle top from Russia, a stone she'd found on a grave in Nepal, an elastic band she'd found on a train floor in Vienna, a brown piece of rope from Iran, a magnifying glass, a notebook for her Big News Diary, and her mother's silver nail varnish.

Ugenia thought about all the exciting things she had managed to do and all the wonderful places she had got to explore: the ice caps, the Incas and India, Olympia, Mount Everest, Morocco and Brazil. And when she wasn't doing that she watched her favourite action hero, Hunk Roberts, in a movie on her mother's laptop. Hunk Roberts was very hunky, and braver than anyone, as he was always going on huge adventures and saving the world.

But now she was on her way to start a new life in England, at a place called Boxmore, which sounded very boring. Ugenia was feeling rather glum.

'Don't worry, you'll like it once we get there,' said her mother, trying to make her feel better.

'Yes, it really is quite nice once you get used to it,' said her father.

Yeah, but what if I don't like 'quite nice'? thought Ugenia, who wasn't so sure about this at all.

Two days later, on Monday morning, 6 January, after driving through more hot, dusty deserts, colourful countries with rocky roads, then taking two boat trips, a train, and one long taxi ride up a very steep hill,

Ugenia and her parents arrived, rather tired, at their new home at 13 Cromer Road. The sky was a murky grey and there was a lethargic drizzle that made everything damp and cold.

Ugenia stared out of the taxicab window at the semi-detached house with its chalky beige bricks, beige-curtained windows and beige front door with a large number thirteen on it. It had a small front garden with an old beige Mini parked on the drive.

'I hate beige,' muttered Ugenia as she peeled herself out from under the suitcases squashed in the taxi. 'I hate the cold, I'm freezing and I wish I was back in Egypt.' Ugenia was still in her explorer shorts, and she shivered as she went to follow her parents up the drive, trying to avoid the dog poo on the pavement.

Ugenia's parents unlocked the door and Ugenia followed them in. She picked up her luminous yellow rucksack, threw it on her back and started to investigate the house . . .

Ugenia stared in dismay at the lounge with its beige carpet and floral wallpaper. The kitchen was also laid out in beige with matching beige and white cupboards, and so was the dining room with its shiny wooden table and lacy tablecloth.

Ugenia sighed dramatically and stomped up the stairs before wandering into her new bedroom. Thankfully it was a medium-sized room, but yet again a very nice shade of BEIGE . . .

Ugenia flopped on the bed and stared at the ceiling. 'I hate my cold, beige new life,' she said, lying quietly for a few moments as her new home became a hive of activity. Ugenia's great-granny, Betty, who lived just around the corner, had come to help them unpack their belongings. Granny Betty was more than just a great-grandmother; she was amazing.

Things you need to know about her:

1. She was 101 years old.

2. She treated every day like Christmas.

3. She gave karate chops to anyone who annoyed her.

And if anyone could make Ugenia feel better about anything, it was Granny Betty.

The next morning, Ugenia was woken by the shrill of her alarm clock. She leaped out of bed as if she was ready to wrestle crocodiles. But then Ugenia remembered where she was, and there wasn't the slightest chance of ever meeting a crocodile in Cromer Road.

Ugenia decided to make the best of things as she wandered into the bathroom and began brushing her teeth, giving herself

a good, confident toothpaste-advert smile in the mirror. She pulled on her most comfortable clothes – jeans, T-shirt and her big comfy boots – ran downstairs and greeted her dad (her mum had already left for work). Then she munched on some burnt toast with peanut butter before throwing on her luminous yellow rucksack. Ugenia was ready for the first day at her new school.

Ugenia got into the beige Mini and her dad drove her down Cromer Road and across Boxmore Hill Green, which was five minutes away from Boxmore Hill Junior School.

'Oh, by the way, I haven't managed to get you the uniform yet,' said her dad. 'You just have to wear a burgundy sweater, but the teacher knows you don't have one yet.'

'A school uniform?' Ugenia gulped as they approached the school gates and parked the car.

Ugenia and Professor Lavender wandered into the red-brick building, down a corridor and into the school's main office.

'This is my daughter, Ugenia Lavender,' said Professor Lavender to a rather round, short woman in a tweed suit, who looked a little bit like a muffin wearing too much rouge. The muffin introduced herself as Mrs Mervin Jones.

'She's starting school today,' Professor Lavender went on. 'I believe she's expected to attend Mrs Flitt's class.'

'Lovely! Follow me, Ugenia,' said Mrs Mervin Jones, who as it turned out was the school secretary.

'OK, Ugenia, well, I'll see you later then,' said her dad.

'OK, bye then,' said Ugenia, trying to be as brave as possible, even though she was feeling rather nervous as she followed the tweed muffin down the wooden corridor towards a large blue door.

Ugenia could hear a rabble of children's voices chuckling and chatting.

Mrs Mervin Jones knocked loudly.

'Enter!' said a voice.

Ugenia followed Mrs Mervin Jones through the blue door and into a room. Suddenly it all went quiet and every single silent face stared at Ugenia.

'Hello, Ugenia . . . I'm Mrs Flitt, your new class teacher,' said Mrs Flitt. 'Everyone please welcome the new girl, Ugenia Lavender, to our class.'

Ugenia stared at the sea of faces, all wearing burgundy sweaters. The faces stared back at Ugenia. There were too many to make out. It just looked like one big burgundy monster with a thousand pairs of eyes staring at her. Suddenly, a screwed-up piece of paper bopped Ugenia on the head and the whole class roared with laughter.

'Stop that at once,' said Mrs Flitt sternly.

Ugenia wished the ground would swallow her up as she stiffened and went bright red.

'Silence! I said that's enough!' shouted Mrs Flitt. 'Ugenia, take a seat at that empty desk at the back.'

Ugenia wandered up through the class to the low whispering of her new, sniggering classmates.

'She looks odd, doesn't she, Sebastian?' said one boy.

'Weird.' Sebastian laughed back.

'Ooh, look at her silly boots, Liberty,' whispered a girl called Anoushka.

'And that hair,' Liberty giggled.

'Well, what do you expect?' said a blonde-haired girl in a very sly, loud voice from the desk next to where Ugenia was about to sit. 'I mean, come on, she is the NEW girl.' The girl looked down her nose at Ugenia. 'Well, hello there, Ugenia, pleased to meet you. I'm Lara. Lara Slater.'

'Er, hello, pleased to meet

you too,' said Ugenia politely.

'How do you know you're pleased to meet me?' said the girl smugly. 'You don't even know me yet! Ah, so you're a know-it-all. I don't like know-it-alls. Oh dear, the new girl is a know-it-all,' she went on, loud enough for some of the class to hear.

'No I'm not. I was just being polite,' said Ugenia quickly.

'Ah, so we have a stuck-up new girl that's a know-it-all. Even better!' said Lara, louder now so that almost half the class could hear.

'I'm not stuck-up,' replied Ugenia, trying not to let this Lara girl get to her. 'Actually I'm very down to earth.'

'Aha, so we have a fake, stuck-up,

know-it-all new girl,' announced Lara, very loud so the whole class could hear.

'OK, class, pay attention,' said Mrs Flitt, who was oblivious to any of what Lara had been saying as she had been frantically looking for her favourite chalk rubber in the stock cupboard. 'We have a full term ahead of us that will really kick off this Saturday with the annual school jumble-sale fete, raising money for blind, disabled dogs in the local community. I want all of you to get into groups and think of different ways to raise money,' continued Mrs Flitt.

Suddenly the class burst into chatter and gathered quickly into their groups.

Lara teamed up with Anoushka and Liberty, Chantelle with Sita and Max. Billy joined Henry and Sebastian, and the rest

of the class seemed to
get with everyone else,
leaving Ugenia all by
herself. Ugenia felt really
awkward, so she lifted
her desk lid up and hid,
pretending to be very busy
fiddling with textbooks
until class was over . . .

☆

Ugenia wandered through her lessons
somewhat aimlessly for the rest of the day,
talking pretty much to no one except a
dinner lady when she asked for mashed
potato, to a girl when she needed to know
where the toilets were and then to Mrs Flitt
when she wanted some paper. The only
person that really spoke to her was Lara

Slater, but they were only rude remarks so that didn't really count. In fact, Lara Slater seemed to make sure no one else came near Ugenia except Lara's two other friends, Liberty and Anoushka, who also joined in with sly, horrible comments.

At the end of the day Ugenia was relieved to get back to 13 Cromer Road, even if it was beige and boring – at least she could relax without feeling different and being made fun of.

Ugenia's parents were still out at work, so Granny Betty was there, waiting to welcome her with a nice cup of tarberry juice and some homemade organic peanut butter and chocolate moon-sludge cookies.

'So, Ugenia, how was it?' asked Granny cheerfully.

'OK, I guess,' said Ugenia, trying not to make a big deal out of her long, dreadful day.

'Hmm, I'm sensing it wasn't the best start you were hoping for,' said Granny Betty, who had a way of reading Ugenia's mind.

'Actually it was a disaster! I hate my life,' said Ugenia, throwing herself on the couch and staring at the ceiling. 'I don't belong here, Gran. I just don't fit in.'

'Yes you do,' said Granny Betty, handing her a burgundy jumper that she had knitted. 'Things will get better, you'll see.

You've just got to stick it out.'

'Thanks, Gran, but if only I was still in Egypt I wouldn't have to face any of this. If we didn't like somewhere we would just move on,' sighed Ugenia sadly.

'Ugenia, everything catches us in the end, no matter how far we run,' explained Granny Betty, who then wandered into the garden.

'Thanks, Gran,' said Ugenia, trying to be grateful as she watched her gran doing wheelies on her red bike outside.

Ugenia then decided that if she couldn't run far away back to Egypt, she could escape by watching one of her favourite Hunk Roberts movies, *The Wasp-eating Killer Water-babies*.

Ugenia tried not to think about having to go back to school the next day and face another round of Lara Slater and her gang of friends. Lara can't get any worse, can she? thought Ugenia. But the very next day that's exactly what Lara did . . .

Lara, who was captain at rounders, made sure Ugenia was the last person to be picked for the team. 'Don't pick that weird new girl,' she laughed. 'She'll be ridiculous – can't you tell?'

And so Ugenia sat on the bench as a

substitute player with a skinny boy called Rudy as she watched the rest of the team wait to bat.

'How come you didn't get picked then?' Ugenia asked the boy.

'I can't play. I've got a sick note from my mother cos I bruised my little toe,' said Rudy.

'How did you do that?' asked Ugenia,

'Oh, it was all in the name of fashion,' beamed Rudy. 'I was trying these amazing shoes on and I tripped.'

'Cool,' said Ugenia, who was just pleased to have a conversation . . .

Ugenia didn't think that the day could get much worse, but at lunch, as she stood in line, queuing up for some shepherd's pie, she was suddenly pelted with cold mushy peas, which splattered over her face. Ugenia felt like a stupid green soggy mess. She looked around her to see Anoushka and Liberty giggling as they proudly waved the offending wooden spoon and half a bowl of mushy peas.

'Ha ha – the new girl looks better in green!' called Lara Slater.

'Injustice!' shouted Ugenia. They were about to splat her with a second helping when she quickly marched off to the toilet.

Ugenia stared in the mirror and began to wipe the mushy green peas from her hair. She was just about to feel sorry for herself when the door swung open and a girl with long dark hair and square glasses wandered in, dripping from head to toe in the same mushy peas.

'They got you as well, huh?' smiled Ugenia, passing her a wet paper towel.

'Yes, you could say I've been mushy-pea-ed too,' laughed the girl shyly. 'I got left in the firing line. Pleased to meet you, Ugenia. I'm Bronte,' she added. 'You know, the only reason Lara is picking on you is because she used to be the new girl in class, which made her special and interesting, but now that you've come along it's spoilt things for her.'

'Oh, right,' said Ugenia, passing Bronte a dry paper towel. 'Well, thanks for telling me that, Bronte, fellow green girl.'

'That's all right,' said Bronte. 'Don't worry about Lara, the worst of it must be over. I'm sure she'll soon get bored with picking on you and find something else for entertainment.'

But as it turned out, that wasn't the case. That afternoon, during English, Lara Slater threw a screwed-up paper at Ugenia, who then threw it back. Ugenia somehow misfired it to land on Mrs Flitt's desk.

'Who threw that?' barked Mrs Flitt.

'The new girl did,' piped up Lara triumphantly.

'Yeah, but, no, but I . . . I,' stammered Ugenia.

'Yes, she did, I saw her,' said Anoushka.

'So did I,' said Liberty.

'INJUSTICE!' shouted Ugenia.

'That's enough – don't raise your voice in my class, young lady,' snapped Mrs Flitt. 'Time out for you. Go and stand in the corridor.'

Double injustice, thought Ugenia as she walked out of the room to an array of giggles.

Ugenia stood in the corridor and stared at a boy opposite who had also been sent out, for sticking gum in a girl's hair.

'All right, what you done?' said the boy, who was known as Crazy Trevor and was slightly chunky with a gruff voice.

'Nothing, I'm innocent,' said Ugenia.

'Er, yeah, me too,' laughed Crazy Trevor.

Ugenia stood outside the class, fuming that things were going from bad to worse, and it was all because of that horrid Lara Slater. But eventually, Ugenia and Crazy Trevor were allowed back into class after a stern talking-to from Mrs Flitt. The teacher reminded everyone that they needed to be working on their ideas for the jumble-sale fete, which would take place in the school gym this Saturday.

After school Ugenia walked home through the rain and wind, which howled with rage as if it knew what Ugenia was feeling.

'Oh, I haven't got anyone to fund-raise with and Lara Slater is making sure it stays that way. What am I going to do?' sighed Ugenia. 'Maybe I should ask my dad? After all, he is a professor and he is very clever and he knows pretty much everything.'

Ugenia jumped on her red bike and sped down Boxmore Hill, past the twenty-four-hour, bargain-budget, bulk-buyers' supersized supermarket and into the town centre. She went straight to the Dinosaur Museum, where her dad worked. It was an old grey building with two stone gargoyles peering down from the roof.

Ugenia wandered through the large, stone building, under the huge diplodocus skeleton, past a stegosaurus horn, down the stairs and along a dusty, dark corridor.

She tiptoed quietly past three men in white coats wearing their do-not-disturb frowns as they peered down at a tiny piece of what looked like dinosaur poo. Ugenia knocked on her father's door, which said:

> PROFESSOR
> # EDWARD LAVENDER
> DINOSAUR CONSULTANT
> ——— AND ———
> SPECIALIST IN PRETTY
> MUCH EVERYTHING ELSE

'Enter!' called Professor Lavender. 'Ah, Ugenia! Is it about that Tyrannosaurus rex tooth I was discussing?'

'Er no, actually it's bigger than that,' said Ugenia, who then told her dad about being bullied by Lara for being the new girl and how it was quite difficult to stand up to her and her two horrid friends.

Professor Lavender knotted his eyebrows together as if they were in deep conversation. 'Hmm, now let me see. Firstly, Lara and her friends sound like a gang of velociraptors. These dinosaurs travel in packs and surround their prey.'

'Great, Dad, but what am I going to do? Apparently the only reason why she is picking on me is because she used to be the new girl and doesn't like it now that I am!' cried Ugenia. 'And I don't even want to be!'

'Aha, I see your dilemma . . . it's a
bit like the rivalry between the Egyptian
queens Cleratoti and Nefranunu, who were
arch-enemies. Nefranunu felt threatened
when Cleratoti came into favour with
King Tata, so she did everything within
her power among her followers to make
everyone hate Cleratoti.

'But Cleratoti was far too smart for
Nefranunu. She made sure she stood
firm and radiated
her own power.
She recruited people
to join her, and
held off any
competition
from her rival,'
said Professor

Lavender, pulling out a book with a large picture of Cleratoti on it, who had black hair and a large headdress and beautiful slanting eyes.

'Ooh, she sounds so cool,' said Ugenia, staring at the powerful Egyptian queen. 'If only I could be like her.'

Then, suddenly, like a thunderbolt of lightning, Ugenia had a brainwave . . .

'Ingenious!' cried Ugenia 'RECRUITMENT! All I need to do is recruit my own tribe to stop Lara Slater being so mean to me! Thanks, Dad.'

'You're welcome. Now, would you like to see that T-rex tooth?'

But Ugenia was already halfway down the corridor.

Before Professor Lavender could say

another word on the matter, Ugenia was pedalling determinedly back up Boxmore Hill. As the rain lashed against her face, Ugenia decided she was going to build her own tribe and show Lara Slater exactly what she was made of, regardless of the weather. Nothing was going to stop her.

The next day at lunch, Ugenia sat down with Rudy. Then Bronte, the mushy-pea girl with glasses, walked passed with her lunch tray.

'Bronte, come and sit with me and Rudy,' smiled Ugenia.

Then Crazy Trevor, with the chunky gruff voice, who she had met in the corridor, plonked himself next to Ugenia, 'Ooh, can I have some of that?' he said, reaching for some of her jam roly-poly before she'd even said yes.

'I'm glad you're all here . . . I have a mission impossible,' announced Ugenia. 'It needs loyalty and dedication and I think you're the best people for the job. I want us to show what we're really made of at the jumble-sale fete for the blind, disabled dogs — together. Like it?'

'Fabulous!' said Rudy.

'Very nice,' said Bronte.

'Er . . . yeah,' said Crazy Trevor.

'I can make a vision board!' shrieked Rudy excitedly.

'What's a vision board?' asked Ugenia.

'Meet me round my house after school and I'll show you!'

☆

And so, after school, Ugenia hopped on her red bike and cycled over to Rudy's house. Rudy lived two streets away on Leavesden Road, where all the houses were stuffed together like cheese and pickle sandwiches. His home was right on the corner above his dad's shop, Patel's Food Store, except it didn't only sell food, it sold newspapers, Sellotape and weird things like pliers.

Five minutes later Crazy Trevor and Bronte appeared, and Rudy's mum offered everyone a glass of tarberry juice and an onion bhaji as they sat up in Rudy's tiny bedroom.

Rudy then pulled out his vision board, which was a large white piece of paper that had lots of writing and diagrams in big black writing. It said:

MISSION IMPOSSIBLE . . .

OUR TRIBE IS THE BEST

LOCATION: SCHOOL GYMNASIUM – BLIND, DISABLED DOGS

FUND-RAISER

DATE: THIS SATURDAY

MISSION IMPOSSIBLE – TO BE THE BEST TRIBAL FUND-

RAISERS EVER!

1. RAFFLE WITH BIG BIG PRIZE: RUDY TO MAKE TICKETS

AND TREVOR TO PROVIDE PRIZE – SOMETHING FROM HIS

GARAGE?

2. GUESS THE WEIGHT OF CAKE: UGENIA TO PROVIDE CAKE.

3. HEAD IN STOCKS: TREVOR HEAD ON A BLOCK. BRONTE

TO PROVIDE BUCKET AND SPONGES.

NB TRIBAL RULE – STICK TOGETHER AND BEAT ANY OTHER

OPPOSITION NO MATTER WHAT.

'Like it?' asked Rudy.

'Love it!' said Ugenia.

'Very nice,' said Bronte.

'Er . . . yeah,' said Crazy Trevor.

The next two days were much easier for Ugenia, as she now had her new tribe of friends to support her. Lara seemed a little less persistent with her horrible comments and, besides, everyone was busy preparing for the jumble-sale fete.

However, on Friday afternoon, when the school bell rang, Ugenia threw on her luminous yellow rucksack and was just about to set off home when she heard a familiar sly voice. It was Lara Slater.

'Well, there she is, the *new* girl, who's actually found some weirdo friends. Actually that reminds me – you can go exactly as you are for the fancy-dress jumble-sale fete tomorrow. You're such a freak, you'll fit right in.'

'Fancy dress? I didn't know it was fancy dress,' said Ugenia.

Lara looked surprised. 'Didn't you? But it's a tradition at this school – everyone who comes to the annual jumble-sale fete always wears fancy dress. Ah well, of course being the *new* girl you can't know everything!' Lara smiled sweetly.

'Ooh, right, thanks,' gulped Ugenia, quickly walking off, not wanting to show her enemy she was bothered.

When Ugenia got home she tried to ring Rudy, Bronte and Trevor to find out what they were wearing, but she didn't manage

to speak to any of them as they were
all out, busy preparing for their mission
impossible – being the best tribe.

Ugenia began to spiral with fear. I'm sick
of being different! she thought as she hid
behind the sofa with worry.

'What are you doing hiding behind
there, Ugenia?' asked Granny Betty.

'Gran, I just can't face my life any
longer,' wailed Ugenia. 'It's not fair – I was
making some progress, now I am gonna be
the freaky new girl again without a fancy-
dress costume.'

'The only thing to fear is fear itself,' said
Granny Betty.

I have no idea what that means, thought
Ugenia, who got up from behind the
sofa, but only because the radiator was

digging into her back.

'You know, Ugenia, playing small, hiding behind the sofa, doesn't help anyone,' explained Granny Betty. 'You have to stand proud and just be exactly who  you are, whatever that looks like. Ooh, by the way, your dad said to take a look at this headdress – he brought it back from the museum. Apparently it's a replica of what the Egyptian queen Cleratoti wore when she finally dethroned Nefranunu.'

Ugenia stared at the large black feathered headpiece with its golden snake finish . . . it looked powerful and enchanting. Suddenly, like a thunderbolt of lightning, Ugenia had a brainwave.

'Ingenius!' cried Ugenia. 'The headpiece! It can be my fancy dress tomorrow when I finally overthrow that horrid Lara!'

'Well, as long as you're careful,' said Granny Betty. 'After all, it does belong to the museum.'

'Sure, I'll be careful, Gran,' grinned Ugenia. 'Besides, this is my one big chance to show Lara Slater that I'm not just some weird new girl that doesn't fit in!' she announced before stomping off to bed with a new gust of hope. Things were so different living in Boxmore. Trying to fit in with everyone at school was exhausting . . .

☆

The next morning Ugenia decided it was time to embrace the day, so she leaped out of bed with her biggest action-hero-Hunk-Roberts leap ever and did a super skydive roll across the carpet, straight to the bathroom. She put on her special queen headdress, gave herself an extra big toothpaste-advert smile in the mirror and brushed her teeth.

It wasn't long before it was time for Ugenia to go to the jumble-sale fete. By midday the school gymnasium was completely full of people bartering over the lucky dips and coconut shies and the vast array of bric-a-brac and clothes. Ugenia walked in, carrying a walnut and mincemeat cake for her fund-raising stall. The cake was as heavy as a brick, but she held her head high, proudly wearing her mother's dressing gown and the museum's

special Egyptian-queen headdress. Ugenia felt very powerful.

Suddenly the noise from all the chattering people stopped . . . there was a loud silence as the whole room stared at Ugenia.

Ugenia grinned. They love my fantastic headdress. I have the best outfit on! she thought, then she heard a rip-roar of laughter and a chorus of giggles from Lara Slater and her friends.

'Nice outfit, you freak new girl!' laughed Lara.

Ugenia looked around the room and realized no one else was wearing any fancy-dress costume at all. Ugenia could feel her face burning with embarrassment. 'Injustice!' she huffed, quickly walking straight to her stall, where Rudy, Bronte and Trevor were setting up. 'Lara told me it was fancy dress!' she cried.

'Don't worry, you look fabulous!' said Rudy, taking the heavy cake from Ugenia and placing it perfectly in the centre of their stall, ready for people to guess its weight. 'And we can show that Lara that we definitely have a better fund-raising tribe than hers.'

At that moment, Lara came over, gave Bronte 10p and grabbed the cake to guess the weight. 'What do I win if I guess it right?'

'Duh, the cake of course!' said Rudy.

Lara began to swing the cake in the air. 'Ooh, it's pretty heavy, isn't it? It weighs a ton!' she said as suddenly she threw it up in the air and then watched it tumble to the ground . . .

SPLAT!

'Ooops! I'm so sorry – I guess it was just much heavier than I thought . . . silly me!' said Lara, walking off proudly.

'I don't believe it . . . she is just awful,' cried Rudy.

'This means war!' said Ugenia.

'But we've still got the raffle and the stocks with wet sponges,' said Bronte.

'Bad news,' said Ugenia. 'It looks like Liberty and Lara have done a raffle too, with a great prize of a cuddly bear.'

'So, Trevor, what did you get as the raffle prize?' asked Rudy.

'Er, I got half a tin of green paint from my dad's garage,' said Trevor. 'He didn't want it so he said I could have it!'

'Half a tin of green paint!' gasped Rudy, 'That's it?'

'Yeah, good, innit? My dad says you only need one coat.'

'Oh no, we're never going to beat the opposition now,' cried Ugenia.

'We've still got the stocks with wet sponges to throw!' said Rudy.

'I've got some more bad news,' said Bronte. 'It looks like Max and Sebastian have their own stocks with wet sponges *and* cream pies to throw – and it's doing very well.'

'Rats!' said Rudy. 'It's so hard to be different!'

'Injustice!' said Ugenia. 'It looks like we're not going to be able to be the best tribe after all.'

Then, suddenly, just as they were about to start packing up their stall, Mrs Mervin Jones, the tweeded muffin school secretary, came over. 'Oooh, Ugenia, what a lovely headdress. May I try it on?'

Ugenia stared at Mrs Mervin Jones, who looked very excited. It was a bit like when Ugenia was travelling around the world and she would want to try out new things that were different from her everyday life. Suddenly, like a thunderbolt of lightning, Ugenia had a brainwave. Inspirational! she thought. The power of the headdress!

'Sure, Mrs Mervin Jones, you can try it on for twenty pence,' said Ugenia. 'Then you'll experience exactly what it feels like to be the queen of Egypt. What a bargain!'

'How fantastic, Ugenia,' said Mrs Mervin Jones, smiling proudly as she stood like a royal tweeded muffin in the Egyptian headdress. Suddenly there was a queue of people, all wanting to have a go and try it on.

'This is great – we're making a fortune for the blind, disabled dogs!' said Rudy.

Suddenly, all her classmates, except for Lara (who was scowling with envy), surrounded Ugenia, commenting on how marvellous and daring it was and how they were definitely the best tribe at fundraising.

'How did you manage to do it?' asked Billy.

'How did you get to be so different?' said Chantelle.

'Well, the thing is . . .' beamed Ugenia, suddenly feeling Lara's eyes burning furiously into her, 'it's pretty easy to be different – especially when you're the *new* girl!'

Big News!

Hello there . . .
I decided I might as well start
my own newsletter. I mean, come
on, you never know – it actually
might get quite exciting here in
Boxmore! Well, it will if I have
anything to do with it . . . ha ha.
Anyway, at least I've made some

new friends . . . actually I love Rudy, Bronte and Crazy Trevor, who is definitely crazy! Rudy is my favourite so far . . .

As for Lara Slater – isn't she just a big horrible cow or what? Such a mean bully – I don't know if any of you have been bullied, but I reckon the best thing to do is not to go through it alone, and so I got my friends to support me.

Lara smashed my cake at the fair – I reckon that was the worst, but you know, good overcame evil and we totally came through, thanks to that fab headdress!

Anyway, I reckon I'm going to

have loads of fun adventures . . .
just you wait. And I hope you stick
around with me to join in.

Big XO
Ugenia Lavender XX

Ingenious Top Tip

Face your fear and feel better!

Look how scared I was about feeling different – I wanted to hide behind the sofa – but thanks to Granny Betty's encouragement, I faced Lara Slater and showed up at school, and look how great it all turned out . . .

2

uGenia Lavender

and the Lovely Illness

It was Tuesday morning.

Ugenia leaped out of bed with even
more enthusiasm than usual. She couldn't
wait to get to school! This was because it
was Valentine's Day next week and Ugenia
had been chosen to be the class Valentine's
Disco Coordinator, which made her feel
very important.

Maybe this year is going to be different,
thought Ugenia, remembering how last

year she didn't get even *one* Valentine's card from any secret admirers.

Surely being Valentine's Disco Coordinator would mean that this year she'd get heaps of cards through her letter box; or maybe even mountains.

Although Ugenia was delighted to be the Valentine's Disco Coordinator, she hadn't quite worked out what the job involved.

At morning break Ugenia recruited her best mates – Rudy, Crazy Trevor and Bronte – to help. Ugenia hadn't known Bronte for very long, but she was becoming Ugenia's NBF (new best friend). Bronte was one of the cleverest girls in the class. She wore square black glasses, she always had her nose in a book and she was very well organized.

'Why don't we start with a theme?' suggested Rudy.

'Very nice,' said Bronte.

'Love it,' said Ugenia.

'Er . . . yeah,' said Trevor.

'I think the theme should be Under the Sea,' suggested Rudy.

'Very nice,' said Bronte.

'Love it,' said Ugenia.

'Er . . . yeah,' said Trevor.

'We could have pink and blue under-the-sea balloons and wear fancy dress,' suggested Rudy.

'Very nice,' said Bronte.

'Love it,' said Ugenia.

'Er . . . yeah,' said Trevor. 'Let's make a humongous tub of fruit punch and have a massive mountain of onion, pepperoni and cheese crisps.'

'Very nice,' said Bronte.

'Love it,' said Ugenia.

Rudy glared at Trevor.

'Er . . . OK,' mumbled Trevor apologetically, 'forget about the crisps.'

'As it's a disco, Ugenia, will there be dancing?' asked Bronte.

'With girls?!' exclaimed Crazy Trevor.

Ugenia nodded.

'Yuck!' cried Trevor. 'That's disgusting!'

'*I'm* a girl. Am *I* disgusting, Trevor?' huffed Ugenia with her hands on her hips.

'Er . . . no,' replied Trevor, looking nervous.

'That's settled then,' said Ugenia. 'Boys and girls will dance together.'

'Who would you like to dance with, Ugenia?' asked Rudy.

'Er . . . I don't know,' lied Ugenia,

picturing Will
Darcy, who she
thought was
as handsome
as action
hero Hunk
Roberts and
ever so dashing.
The problem was
– so did every other
girl in the class, so
Ugenia felt like she had
no chance with Darcy
and besides, he never
even seemed to notice her.

'How are we going to get everyone to
dance with each other?' asked Bronte.

Ugenia thought about this – it could be a

problem, as some boys and girls wouldn't be seen dead dancing together.

Ugenia, Rudy, Crazy Trevor and Bronte were all silent for a while.

Then suddenly, like a thunderbolt of lightning, Ugenia had a brainwave.

'Ingenious!' cried Ugenia. 'A DANCING-COUPLES COMPETITION! There'll be prizes and awards and trophies!'

'Very nice!' cried Bronte.

'Love it!' Rudy agreed, beaming.

'Er . . . yeah, OK,' said Trevor.

'Let's make posters and pin them up everywhere!' shouted Ugenia.

Immediately the four of them set to work on the posters.

Ugenia ran around the school, putting up as many posters as she could. Then she went to lunch.

As she stood in line holding a tray of shepherd's pie and waiting for a portion of jam roly-poly, Ugenia imagined gliding around the room with Will Darcy at the Valentine's Disco.

Ugenia was deep in thought when there in front of her was Darcy himself.

Immediately her heart began to thump like a drum, her knees became two wibbly-wobbly jellies and she dropped her shepherd's pie on to Darcy's gleaming brown shoes.

Ugenia's face went bright red.

'Oh . . . oh . . . oh my gosh, D–D–Darcy!' she stuttered. 'I am s–s–SO sorry!'

'It's OK,' said Darcy, smiling and wiping the shepherd's pie off his gleaming brown shoes with a serviette.

Ugenia hurried away and joined her friends.

'Hey, Ugenia,' said Rudy.

'You look weird,' said Trevor.

'Is something wrong?' asked Bronte.

'It's nothing,' replied Ugenia. 'I just feel a bit dizzy.'

She picked up her fork, poked her jam roly-poly and stared into space.

'Mission Control to Ugenia,' said Rudy. 'What's up with you?'

'Yeah,' nodded Crazy Trevor, eyeing up her roly-poly.

'I'm just not hungry today,' sighed Ugenia dreamily.

'So you won't mind if
I eat your jam roly-
poly,' said Trevor,
stuffing the whole
thing into his
mouth in one go.

That afternoon Ugenia decided to put up
some more posters by the lockers.

She was standing on a stool when she
heard a smooth, familiar voice. It was Will
Darcy.

'Hi, Ugenia, I hope you managed to
have some lunch.' Will smiled at her.

Immediately, Ugenia's heart began to
thump like a drum, her knees became two
wibbly-wobbly jellies and she fell off the
stool, crashing down straight on to Darcy.

Ugenia's face went bright red.

'Oh . . . oh . . . oh my gosh, D-D-Darcy!' she stuttered, 'I am s-s-SO sorry!'

'It's OK,' said Darcy, smiling and removing a Valentine's poster that was wrapped around his head.

Ugenia hurried away to get some more posters. She had just collected some Blu-Tack when she felt a tap on her shoulder.

She turned round and came face to face with Henry from her drama class. 'Can I ask you something about the Valentine's Disco?' said Henry.

'Maybe later,' answered Ugenia, 'after I've finished putting all these posters up.'

And with that, Ugenia walked off.

What's wrong with me? wondered Ugenia. Why do I feel so peculiar?

The peculiar feeling didn't go away. Ugenia was still feeling it two days before the Valentine's Disco.

Maybe I should ask my dad, thought Ugenia. After all, he is a professor and he is very clever and he knows pretty much everything.

After school Ugenia jumped on her red

71

bike and sped down Boxmore Hill, past the twenty-four-hour, bargain-budget, bulk-buyers' supersized supermarket and into the town centre.

She went straight to the Dinosaur Museum.

Ugenia wandered through the large, stone building, under the huge diplodocus skeleton, past a stegosaurus horn, down the stairs and along a dusty, dark corridor.

She tiptoed quietly past three men in white coats wearing their do-not-disturb frowns as they peered down intently at a tiny piece of what looked like a dinosaur wart. Ugenia knocked on her father's door, which said:

PROFESSOR
EDWARD LAVENDER
DINOSAUR CONSULTANT
— AND —
SPECIALIST IN PRETTY
MUCH EVERYTHING ELSE

'Enter!' called Professor Lavender.

'Hi, Dad,' said Ugenia, bursting in. 'I really need your help.'

'Is this about that brontosaurus nostril?' asked her father, giving Ugenia a kind smile.

'No,' said Ugenia. 'I think I might be ill.'

'What are your symptoms?' enquired Professor Lavender.

'Well, my heart beats like a drum, my legs become wibbly-wobbly jellies and I seem to lose my balance whenever I see this boy called Will Darcy.'

Professor Lavender looked intently at his daughter for a few seconds and then burst out laughing.

'What are you laughing at?' snapped Ugenia. 'This is not a laughing matter!'

'It sounds to me,' said Ugenia's father, trying not to smile, 'as if you have a bad case of what's known as the Lovely Illness.'

'The Lovely Illness?' gasped Ugenia. 'Is it serious? Is it contagious? Is there a cure?'

'It's not serious,' he replied, 'it can be a little contagious, and as far as I know there's no cure.'

'NO CURE?' cried Ugenia.

'I'm afraid so,' he replied softly. 'I think you're Love Sick.'

'So what am I going to do?'

Professor Lavender thought hard for a couple of minutes and his eyebrows nudged each other. Then suddenly his face brightened up.

'The female praying mantasaurus always conquers this Lovely Illness nonsense by directly chasing and trapping her ideal mate,' he said. 'The male of her species is drawn towards her intoxicating scent and thus can't avoid her. Once he has fallen for her, she eats him up and is done with him.'

At that second, like a thunderbolt of lightning, Ugenia had a brainwave.

'INGENIOUS!' cried Ugenia. 'Entrapment! I'll set a trap for Darcy!'

'Great!' Professor
Lavender
beamed.
'Would you
like to see that
brontosaurus
nostril now?'

But Ugenia
didn't hear him.
She was already halfway down the
corridor.

The next day at lunch, while Ugenia was
sitting in the canteen waiting for Rudy,
Crazy Trevor and Bronte to arrive, she
suddenly saw Darcy approaching.

Ugenia panicked and quickly dived
under the table.

She tried to calm herself, but the Lovely Illness was taking over again. Her heart started to beat like a drum and her legs became two wibbly-wobbly jellies.

'Can I ask you something about the Valentine's Disco?' said Henry, peering down at Ugenia.

'Maybe later,' interrupted Ugenia, 'after I've finished hiding under this table.'

And at that, Henry walked off.

Ugenia waited under the table for a long time, but her friends didn't show up.

As Ugenia sat under the table feeling miserable, she suddenly remembered something she'd seen in a Hunk Roberts film. In *The Jungle of Mutant Mountain Mumbersnakes*, the temptress Kinvara Honey lays a trap to capture Hunk Roberts. First she entrances him with her big eyes and then she leaves a secret message for him . . . Soon he is besotted with her.

'INSPIRATIONAL!' cried Ugenia. 'Entrancement! I'll entrance Darcy with my big eyes and, if that doesn't work, I'll send him a secret message. Then maybe he'll ask me to be his Valentine's Disco dancing partner.'

Feeling a sudden boost of confidence, Ugenia leaped out from under the table and immediately spotted Will Darcy eating his lunch.

Ugenia ignored her thumping-like-a-drum heartbeat and wibbly-wobbly-jelly legs and gave Darcy the biggest eyes she could manage.

'Hey, Ugenia,' said Darcy with a puzzled expression, 'what's wrong with your eyes?'

'Er . . . nothing,' lied Ugenia. 'They're just a bit sore.'

'I have some eye drops in my rucksack,' said Darcy, peering deeply into Ugenia's eyes. He took out a little blue bottle of Refreshtickle eye drops and gave them a gentle squirt into Ugenia's big eyes.

'Er, thanks. That's much better,' said Ugenia.

The big eyes didn't work, thought Ugenia. I'll have to try Kinvara

Honey's other technique – a secret message.

It took a few goes before she got it right:

1. I think you're almost as handsome as Hunk Roberts.

Nah, too cheesy.

2. I love the fact that you carry eye drops around.

Nah, too medical.

3. What are you doing tomorrow afternoon? Are you going to the Valentine's Disco and do you have a partner yet? If you don't, perhaps I could be your partner. Of course, that's only if you want to – unless you're doing something else.

Nah, too silly.

4. Be my Valentine . . . Love
from the Valentine's Disco
Coordinator.

That's it! A simple clue!

Ugenia wrote this down on a yellow Post-it
note and slipped it into Will Darcy's locker.

She felt a rush of excitement and nerves.
Her tummy began to wash around like
spaghetti in a tumble dryer. She went to
search for Rudy, Crazy Trevor and Bronte.
Where were they anyway?

Ugenia finally found them in the school
gymnasium. Bronte was wrapping a chair
in foil, Rudy was decorating the gym
equipment with baby-blue toilet roll, and
Crazy Trevor was at the top of a climbing
rope, hanging paper fish on the ceiling.

Henry was also there, polishing the floor with his mother's dishcloth.

'We're creating that under-the-sea effect!' gushed Rudy when he spotted Ugenia. 'Isn't it gorgeous?'

'Wow!' marvelled Ugenia (feeling a bit miffed that they'd got on with the decorations without her).

'We thought you'd given up the Valentine's Disco Coordinator job, so

Bronte's taken over,' said Trevor.

'I hope you don't mind me helping out,' said Bronte. 'It's just that we needed to get things done and you didn't seem to be . . . here.'

'Thanks a lot,' Ugenia muttered, frowning. She was suddenly feeling very unimportant, and stormed out.

'Touchy!' said Crazy Trevor, swinging upside down on the rope.

The next day was 14 February – Valentine's Day. Ugenia had had no reply to the note she'd put in Darcy's locker.

She felt particularly glum at breakfast. The disco was that afternoon and she didn't have anyone to dance with.

'Not working out as you hoped?' asked her dad.

Ugenia shook her head.

'Perhaps you need to take a leaf out of the pteranodon's book – she flies proud and solo,' offered her dad.

'INNOVATIVE!' cried Ugenia. 'Fly proud and solo!'

There was no use having a pity party, she decided, so she ran upstairs and put on her flying mermaid outfit with sequinned wings.

It won't be such a big deal, Ugenia reassured herself that afternoon. I'll just

dance with my friends.
Ugenia had to admit
that the gym looked
amazing, with an
inflatable octopus,
a solar-powered
shipwreck,
piranha-eating
sea horses and a
vast tub of fizzy blue Ocean Punch.

'Welcome to my world!' beamed Rudy
as he swept Miss Medina, one of the
teachers, round the dance floor.

Ugenia peered round the room and saw
that everyone else was also dancing with a
partner.

Sita was dancing with Max.

Cara was dancing with Billy.

Sebastian was dancing with Chantelle and Liberty.

Even Trevor was dancing (very reluctantly) with Anoushka.

And then, to Ugenia's horror, she saw that Bronte was dancing with WILL DARCY!

'INJUSTICE!' cried Ugenia. 'Why are they together? They don't even look happy about it!'

'Darcy wanted to dance with the Valentine's Disco Coordinator, because she sent him a special message,' explained Henry, suddenly appearing at Ugenia's side. 'I told him it was Bronte, and I'm gutted because I wanted to dance with her. I've been trying to get your help with asking her for ages.'

'INCREDIBLE!' cried Ugenia. 'MULTI-MIX-UP! That's why Darcy and Bronte are so miserable! I think I can sort it out though,' she said. 'Follow me!'

She marched straight over to Bronte and Darcy, dragging Henry with her.

'Will,' announced Ugenia when she

reached them, 'I'm actually the Valentine's Disco Coordinator. I wrote you the note. You're meant to be dancing with me.'

Ugenia then shoved Henry towards Bronte.

'Very nice,' said Bronte.

'Like it,' said Henry.

'Love it,' said Ugenia.

'It's dancing-couples competition time!'

declared Miss Medina. 'If I tap you on the shoulder, you and your partner must leave the dance floor. The last couple left are the winners!'

'Come on!' shouted Ugenia, grabbing Darcy by the arm. 'Let's dance!'

Everyone jumped on to the dance floor and began dancing to a song called 'Swim to the shore with my baby'.

Ugenia was delighted, as her Kinvara Honey trap had worked! She flew round the dance floor with Will Darcy.

Miss Medina kept tapping lots of people on their shoulders.

Three and a half minutes later, Ugenia realized that she and Darcy were the only couple left.

'Ugenia and Will are the winners!'

announced Miss Medina.

'DOUBLE INCREDIBLE!' cried Ugenia.

Ugenia and Darcy were given their crowns and trophies and they took their places on the golden Neptune thrones.

Ugenia felt very, very important.

'Isn't this the best Valentine's Day ever, Darcy?' said Ugenia, beaming.

'Darcy?'

But Will Darcy didn't reply. He was sitting on his throne, staring at Ugenia with a glazed expression on his face.

'Are you all right?' Ugenia asked.

'I-I . . . f-f-f-f-feel a bit funny.' Darcy stared dreamily at Ugenia. 'My heart is beating l-l-like a drum and my l-l-legs feel like wibbly-wobbly jellies.'

'It's not serious,' Ugenia said, grinning. 'It's just the Lovely Illness!'

Big News!

Hi there, everyone!
OK, just wanted to let you
know I'm feeling so much better
after that Lovely Illness. I did feel
really weird, so be careful – it's
contagious! Just you wait until it
happens to you – then you'll know
what I mean!!

Anyway, this is a super-duper quickie, cos I'm busy stuffing my rucksack with as much as poss. I mean, you never know when you might need something, do you? So I've packed my mother's new silver nail polish. She wears it on her TV show . . . you might've seen her on *Breakfast TV* when she's waving her hands around a lot? And I've packed some golden-nutty-cornflake sandwiches and some cucumber slices for either snacking on or to put on puffy eyes (that's the cucumber slices NOT the sandwiches!).

I'm thinking I have to try and

look my best so I feel good inside AND out.

Gotta run . . . my dad wants me to go to the museum with him. I'm going to help him polish his latest dinosaur bone . . . Cool!

Big XO
Ugenia Lavender XX

Ingenious Top Tip

The path of true love never runs straight

My great-gran told me this.
I think it means that sometimes
things can get a bit difficult,
but they usually turn out all right
in the end. A bit like me and
Darcy!

3

uGenia Lavender

The Glass Licker

Ugenia rolled out of bed and stared through the window ready for action as she assessed what kind of day it was going to be. It wasn't like Egypt, where Ugenia had lived before and which was always so hot and colourful. The English weather had a mind of its own – one day it was having a tantrum and pouring with rain, the next there was a brief moment of sparkling sunshine just to tease you.

But today it was one of those days when the weather just couldn't make up its mind at all – actually nor could the season. It wasn't exactly freezing, but there wasn't the promise of spring either. Ugenia frowned. Hmm, this weather is just dull – boring and beige, like this house, she thought as she stared at her wallpaper, which had remained a nice shade of beige since she had moved here in January. Her parents had bought her a fantastic Hunk Roberts action-hero bedspread though, which did liven things up a little bit.

It was Saturday and Ugenia hadn't anything special planned, so she decided to watch a repeat of a Hunk Roberts movie. She could watch the same movie over and over again if he was in it. He was always so brave and would turn any horrid situation around into something positive. Ugenia went to put one of her favourite movies on: *The Revenge of the Yellow Golden Spud Thief*, which was about an evil villain who robbed lots of banks and would always leave a golden potato as his trademark. Hunk Roberts was desperate to try and catch him.

But when Ugenia went to put the DVD on, it wouldn't work. In fact, the DVD player was jammed with one of her  dad's dinosaur documentaries.

'Injustice!' groaned Ugenia. 'Now what

am I going to do?'

Ugenia then went downstairs and stared at her parents, who were busy chatting enthusiastically about where in the hall to hang a picture of an African bull elephant.

'I think it belongs right in the middle,' said Professor Lavender.

'No, hang it in the bathroom,' said her mother.

'What do you think, Ugenia?' asked her father.

Ugenia shrugged her shoulders as if to say, 'I don't really care.' Then she announced, 'I think it will look good anywhere. To be honest, this house is so drab it needs cheering up with as many colourful pictures as possible.'

'I think she's got a point,' said her dad. 'Let's decorate the hall!'

'If we're going to start decorating anywhere at all, I think we should start with the kitchen,' said her mum.

'How about my bedroom?' interrupted Ugenia.

'Yes! Why don't we go to the DIY store together and choose paints . . . as a family outing!' Pandora announced enthusiastically (she was actually a DIY fanatic).

'Boring!' sighed Ugenia as she rolled her eyes in desperation. Going to the DIY store, staring at paint pots, was as boring as watching paint dry, she thought.

Just as Ugenia was desperately trying to think of a cunning plan to avoid going, the doorbell rang . . .

It was Uncle Harry, Professor Lavender's brother, who was a celebrity chef and taught people how to cook on television by shouting at them.

'Ooh I am so glad you're here. I'm so streeeeesssssed out. I've been working on trying to perfect a spaghetti tomato-sauce recipe and I just can't seem to get it right!' said Harry, pulling a very stressed-out face and holding his head. 'And it has to be perfect. Do you know how hard it is to be perfect?'

'Ooh dear, let me get you a nice glass of tarberry juice,' said Pandora. 'Ugenia get your uncle a glass of tarberry juice.'

104

'I'm not a slave,' huffed Ugenia as she strutted to the kitchen to get the drink.

When Ugenia returned to the lounge, where her parents and Uncle Harry were sitting, her uncle had his head in his hands and seemed to be puffing and sighing a lot.

'Ugenia, we have an excellent idea,' said her mother. 'We can tell you're not exactly thrilled to go to the DIY store with us so you're going to do something far more exciting!'

'We would like you to spend some quality time with your Uncle Harry,' said her dad. 'He needs a little bit of relaxation and time out today, so we've come up with the perfect solution.'

'Yes, Ugenia, you lucky girl,' smiled Uncle Harry, who seemed to be calming down a bit. 'You and I are going to take in some marvellous art at the gallery in Boxmore Town Centre.'

'Isn't that great?' smiled Pandora. 'You wanted to see a bit of vibrant colour and now that's exactly what you'll get!'

Ugenia slung on her luminous yellow rucksack and shrugged her shoulders. 'Great, I'm ready. Let's go then. Anything is better than staring at these four beige walls,' she muttered under her breath.

Ugenia waved goodbye to her parents as she put on a big crash helmet and got in the sidecar of Uncle Harry's golden Harley-Davidson motorbike.

Uncle Harry zipped up his leather jacket then turned on the engine, which purred like a tiger ready to pounce.

106

'Now, have fun!' said her parents, smiling.

Ugenia and Uncle Harry sped down Boxmore Hill, past the twenty-four-hour, bargain-budget, bulk-buyers' supersized supermarket and into the town centre. They passed the Dinosaur Museum and started to slow down as they approached a large white symmetrical building with gleaming glass

doors and a big shiny sign: THE WHITE
BOX – Boxmore Art Gallery. Uncle Harry

THE WHITE BOX

screeched
on his
brakes
and
parked his
bike right
outside.

'Is it
all right
to park
here?' said
Ugenia,

who was pretty sure you weren't allowed to
park on double yellow lines.

'Yes, it's fine. I really can't be dealing
with any hassle. Let's not worry about

those petty things today – we're here to relax, remember! Besides it's only MY little bike,' said Uncle Harry, removing his shiny helmet and black shades.

Ugenia followed Uncle Harry up the white staircase, through the glass doors and into a pristine gigantic white hall.

Uncle Harry went up to the reception desk. 'We have come to look around,' he announced.

'Great, sir . . . you're just in time,' said the girl behind the desk. 'A tour will be starting in three minutes. You can join in!'

'Join in?' squirmed Uncle Harry. 'That sounds very stressful.'

But before Uncle Harry had any time to complain, a very tall man wearing black-framed glasses came into the hall followed by a large crowd of Japanese people with lots of cameras and hats and bags and stuff.

'Good morning! My name is Mr Poplin. Welcome to my world – The White Box!' he announced as the Japanese people began snapping away frantically at him. Mr Poplin owned the art gallery and loved art.

'Now today, ladies and gentlemen,' continued Mr Poplin, 'you will be privileged to see the finest collection of art in the world, ranging from ancient treasures to the new and directional pieces from our biggest names in Boxmore. These paintings are worth millions of pounds, so no touching!' laughed Mr Poplin as he brushed a piece of dust from his purple velvet suit.

Uncle Harry and Ugenia followed Mr

Poplin and the crowd
of Japanese people
through the gallery.
Each room was
white with tall
ceilings and huge,
spacious walls
with one picture
on each of them.
Finally they came
to a stop.

'Ah, now this is a
masterpiece,' said Mr Poplin, pointing to
a statue of a man with no clothes on and
with an arm missing.

'Aha!' nodded the Japanese people with
delight, snapping away with their cameras.

Mr Poplin led them on again. 'And this

is just wonderful,' he announced, pointing to a painting. 'Probably the best piece of modern art created in Boxmore by the artist Damian Burst. It's absolute perfection!'

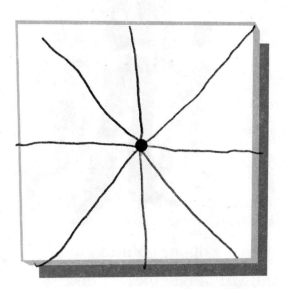

Ugenia stared at the large canvas with a small yellow dot in the middle. 'Anyone could do that in five minutes. It looks easy,' she said.

'Ah, but it's a conceptual directional vision of space and colour,' said Mr Poplin.

'Oh, really, how fascinating,' said Ugenia,

who had no idea what this man was talking about. 'I still reckon I could do it though!'

'Nonsense, it's perfection! It took him years,' said Mr Poplin.

'Yeah, right,' smirked Ugenia (who actually thought it was a load of old pap).

'Oh, don't mind her,' Uncle Harry chipped in. 'She doesn't understand art, that's all,' he said, beginning to get a bit stressed as the Japanese people continued to snap away.

Mr Poplin waved everyone on. 'Now, I need your attention,' he announced. 'Would you all put your cameras down. No pictures allowed for the next masterpiece we are about to see – it's the most famous painting in the whole world ever . . . it's called the *Dona Plisa* . . .'

Mr Poplin led them forward to where a
painting was hanging on its own behind
a thick piece of glass. It was of a dark-
haired woman who was sort of smiling.
Ugenia stared at it.

'Now you may
notice she has a
very bemused,
puzzling smile,' Mr
Poplin went on.
'Apparently it's
because she was

holding a big secret, and the reason why
the painting is behind that glass is so that no
one can touch it, because its worth at least
ten squillion pounds!'

The crowd gasped and gathered around
the painting as they all tried to take a look

at the squillion-pound bemused, puzzling smile.

'Oh, I can't see a thing with all these irritating people,' snapped Uncle Harry as an old woman elbowed him out of her way for a closer look at the painting.

Ugenia noticed that Uncle Harry was beginning to pull the same stressed-out face he had when he arrived at Ugenia's home earlier. Ugenia sensed this was getting a bit much for her uncle . . .

'Look, why don't we get some fresh air,' she said. 'All this art is a lot to take in – we can come back in a bit.'

'What a good idea,' said Uncle Harry. 'You really do take after the Lavender side of the family.'

Ugenia and Uncle Harry retraced their

steps back out through The White Box gallery, down the steps and on to the pavement. Ugenia stared at the white van parked outside on the double yellow line.

'Uncle Harry, where's your bike?' she cried. 'Isn't that where we left it?'

'Oh dear . . . no no . . . not my dear precious baby . . . golden goddess . . . it's been stolen!' cried Uncle Harry.

At that moment a traffic warden appeared at their side. 'It hasn't been stolen,' he announced as he vigorously wrote out a ticket for the white van. 'It's been towed for parking on a double yellow line.'

'Outrageous!' said Uncle Harry.

'Injustice!' said Ugenia. 'Don't worry, Uncle Harry, we'll get her back!'

A black cloud appeared in the sky, grumbling as if it agreed with them, and then it began to rain.

'Ooh, I don't feel well. My stress levels are rising!' said Uncle Harry as he leaned back on the white van and held his head in despair. Then, suddenly, the back door of the white van swung open . . .

Ugenia grabbed Uncle Harry's hand and pulled him inside the van. 'Let's just take five minutes' time out so we don't get wet, sit quietly and think about what to do.'

'Good idea,' said Uncle Harry, who was now starting to huff and pant.

So Ugenia and Uncle Harry climbed inside the back of the empty white van, sat down and made themselves comfortable before shutting the van door.

Uncle Harry put his head in his hands.

'You know, Ugenia, it's not easy being me . . . it's so much pressure trying to create the perfect spaghetti tomato sauce.'

Ugenia and Uncle Harry sat in silence for a few minutes as Uncle Harry began to calm down . . .

Then suddenly there was the sound of a loud alarm followed by raised voices. The back of the van door swung open and a painting was thrown in. Then the van door was quickly slammed shut. It happened so fast Ugenia had no time to see who it was that threw the painting in. Whoever shut the door climbed into the front seat and then the engine spluttered into life and the van quickly sped off. Ugenia and Uncle Harry were flung

forward as the van flew through the town.

'What is going on?' demanded Uncle Harry to the man sitting in the driver's seat, who was wearing a black balaclava so his face couldn't be seen.

The man began talking very quickly in a language that sounded familiar to Ugenia but that she couldn't understand, then he started speaking English.

'Shush, be quiet,' he said in a foreign accent.

'I demand to know exactly what is going on,' shouted Uncle Harry. 'Let us out immediately!'

The man in the balaclava stared back at Uncle Harry in his rear-view mirror with dark 'don't mess with me' eyes.

Uncle Harry gave a worried look to Ugenia, but Ugenia just stared out of the window, listening to the faint sound of police sirens in the distance.

'I'm afraid I can't let you out right now,' said the man in the black balaclava. 'I'm in a hurry.'

'I think he's a robber, Uncle Harry,' whispered Ugenia, who recognized that the black balaclava was the same sort as the one the yellow golden-spud-thief villain wore in the Hunk Roberts movie, and he too spoke in the same weird language.

'Now, what makes you think that?' sighed Uncle Harry. 'I really can't deal with robbers . . . it's not good for my stress levels . . . he's probably just trying to avoid being towed off by the traffic warden.'

Ugenia stared at the painting that had been thrown in the back. It was of the dark-haired woman, who was now giving Ugenia the bemused, puzzling smile.

'I definitely think he's a robber, Uncle Harry . . . unless he has just borrowed the painting of the *Dona Plisa*,' said Ugenia.

The man in the balaclava began to talk even faster in his foreign language as the van sped out to the edge of town. They could no longer hear any sirens as they drove through a vast wasteland and into a big warehouse.

'I think he could be Russian, Uncle Harry,' whispered Ugenia. 'Just like the villain in the Hunk Roberts movie.'

'Well done, very smart,' said Uncle Harry, who was now sweating.

'OK, follow me,' said the Russian man in the balaclava as he opened the back of the van door.

'I think we'd better do what he says just for now,' said

Uncle Harry. 'Don't worry, you'll be safe with me. I'll protect you.'

'Wow, this is just like a real Hunk Roberts movie . . . I think he might even keep us captive with bread and water and maybe even torture us. What do you reckon, Uncle Harry?' said Ugenia.

'Let's not get hasty,' said Uncle Harry, who was now sweating even more.

Uncle Harry and Ugenia followed the man through the warehouse, which was cold and grey and seemed to have no doors or windows.

The man then pressed a button on the wall and a metal slatted shutter began to elevate . . . revealing a door.

Uncle Harry and Ugenia were led into a small room with grey walls and one small window. The room was completely empty except for some old decorating materials, a wallpapering table and some paints and brushes.

Uncle Harry and Ugenia gulped as the door slammed shut behind them and they were locked in . . .

'Well, I guess you wanted some time out for rest and relaxation,' said Ugenia, trying to make her uncle feel a bit better.

Ugenia was feeling a bit scared, but she didn't want to stress out her uncle any more than he already was.

Uncle Harry and Ugenia sat back to back in the middle of the room, as all the walls were a bit dirty and Uncle Harry didn't want to get his clothes mucky. Ugenia stared at the window and tried to

think of ways they could escape.

'Uncle Harry, do you have your mobile? We could call the police,' said Ugenia.

'Bother, I haven't got it,' Uncle Harry sighed. 'The people from my cooking show kept bugging me for the new spaghetti tomato-sauce ingredient and I just couldn't face them today, so I left my mobile in my motorbike trunk. Oh, stupid me . . . it's all my fault. If only I wasn't so obsessed with trying to find the perfect spaghetti tomato sauce we wouldn't be in this mess in the first place. I'm so sorry, Ugenia.'

'Don't worry about it,' said Ugenia. 'Spaghetti sauce should be taken seriously! I'm working on being the perfect spaghetti taster and tomato sauce is an important part of spaghetti, so I totally understand, Uncle Harry. I was only going to a DIY store with Mum and Dad, so it looks like I've ended up staring at pots and paints in the end anyway.'

Ugenia stared out of the small window and watched the rain fall freely. She felt really glum. What was going to happen to her and Uncle Harry? Would they be locked in this room forever? It was really dull just sitting there doing nothing.

Ugenia stared at the old paint pots and opened her luminous yellow rucksack, taking out a mini screwdriver she had borrowed from her dad. She opened one of the paint pots. 'Look, Uncle Harry, it's half full,' said Ugenia, showing Uncle Harry half a tin of red paint.

'Half empty, you mean,' frowned Uncle Harry, still thinking about perfecting spaghetti tomato sauce.

'Well, it depends how you look at it, doesn't it?' said Ugenia as she climbed on the wallpapering table, dipped a large paintbrush in the red paint and painted a humongous red squiggly circle on the wall. She then opened another can of paint and did one big yellow splat in the middle of the circle. Ugenia smiled at the red squiggle with the yellow splat.

'There you go, Uncle Harry, a visual

feast of spaghetti perfection!' giggled Ugenia.

Uncle Harry stared at the red squiggly circle with the yellow splat in the middle.

'Very inspirational,' smiled Uncle Harry, who was slightly cheering up.

Ugenia and Uncle Harry were both feeling rather hot because, although it was quite cool outside, it was quite stuffy in the room as there was no fresh air.

'I'm so thirsty' said Uncle Harry.

'Me too,' said Ugenia, staring at the one small window, which was now misting up with beads of water caused by the heat in the room. 'We really need to look after ourselves,' she added as she tried to open the window. 'Hunk Roberts always keeps his strength up, especially when he's in a jam.' The trickles of water were beginning to look rather appealing to Ugenia.

Then suddenly, like a thunderbolt of lightning, Ugenia had a brainwave. 'Ingenious! Glass lick!'

Ugenia stretched up to the windowpane,

gave it a lick and smiled.

'Hmm, come on, Uncle Harry,' she cried, suddenly feeling a bit better. 'Come and be a glass licker! It tastes all right!'

'Very well, but has my life really come to this – being a glass licker?' sighed Uncle

Harry, who was looking rather flustered and hot as he slowly walked up to the window. Ugenia's uncle then gave the window one enormous lick . . .

'Hmm, not bad!' he laughed. 'You're right, Ugenia, this condensation tastes good!'

Uncle Harry, feeling revitalized, gave the window a shove and it popped open. The two revitalized glass lickers stuck their heads out of the small window and breathed in the fresh air, enjoying the feeling of a refreshing drizzle of rain spitting on their faces.

'Ah, that's even better!' said Ugenia.

The grey clouds gave a final little spit and then a large multicoloured rainbow appeared, gleaming across the blue sky.

Ugenia breathed in the hopeful sunlight
and, for a brief moment, she almost forgot
that she and Uncle Harry were imprisoned
in a horrible stuffy room. Then suddenly
Ugenia could hear a deep, husky Russian
voice . . . the *Dona Plisa* thief was coming.

'Quick, Uncle Harry, we have to do
something,' whispered Ugenia.

Without a moment's thought,
Uncle Harry and Ugenia dragged the
wallpapering table to the side of the door
and climbed on it,
each armed with
a half-full tin of
red paint. Just as
the door swung
open, Uncle Harry
and Ugenia both

threw their tins of red paint and splattered
the *Dona Plisa* thief (who was still wearing a
black balaclava).

The *Dona Plisa* thief was so stunned he
fell back on to the floor.

Without a moment to lose, Uncle Harry
and Ugenia quickly jumped off the table
and ran out of the room, leaving the
Russian balaclava-wearing *Dona Plisa* thief
dazed and confused in
a heap, splattered in
red paint.

Ugenia and
Uncle Harry
dashed through
the warehouse
towards the
white van. They

jumped in the front and Uncle Harry
quickly started the engine.

The engine erupted and they sped out of
the warehouse, across the wasteland and
headed back to the town centre right back
to the Boxmore art gallery. Just as they
were parking, Ugenia peered over into the
back of the van and to her surprise there in
the back was the painting of the woman
with the dark hair and very bemused,
puzzling smile.

'Incredible!' gasped Ugenia. 'It's safe!'

Ugenia and Uncle Harry walked back
into the gallery, proudly returning the
squillion-pound bemused, smiling *Dona Plisa*
to Mr Poplin, who welcomed them with a
big crowd of excited onlookers.

Mr Poplin was so pleased to have the

133

painting back that he immediately arranged
to get Uncle Harry's Harley-Davidson
bike returned as a thank-you, as well as a
lifetime's free membership to The White
Box gallery.

Uncle Harry and Ugenia jumped on the
bike and roared back up Boxmore Hill to
Cromer Road. As they walked up the path
to the house, Ugenia's parents were there to
greet them.

'How was it? Did you have a lovely
relaxing afternoon?' said Professor
Lavender.

'Well, I'm not stressed out any more,'
said Uncle Harry. 'The afternoon certainly
did the trick in distracting me from the
importance of perfection, that's for sure!
Thanks to Ugenia, maybe it's time I started

looking at my tomato-sauce recipe a bit
differently. It's almost perfect, rather than
not quite right!'

After Ugenia and Uncle Harry told her
parents about their afternoon adventure,
Ugenia got another surprise when she was
led up to her bedroom – her parents had
been doing a bit of painting themselves and
had painted her room electric blue with a
big rainbow stripe.

'Exceptional!' said Ugenia gratefully.
'Much better than boring beige!'

A week later Ugenia and Uncle Harry
were invited to The White Box gallery to a
new exhibition where a famous artist was
going to be unveiling his new painting.
As they walked into the building, which

was heaving with people, Mr Poplin was standing in front of a large red curtain.

'Ladies and gentlemen,' he announced. 'May I have your attention. It gives me great pleasure to introduce a new Russian artist – a total genius. Here is his first masterpiece.'
And, pulling back the red curtain, Mr Poplin revealed a large painting of a humongous squiggly red circle with a big yellow splat in the middle!

'So what do you think, Miss Ugenia Lavender . . . could *anybody* paint such perfection in five minutes?' laughed Mr Poplin.

Ugenia stared at the humongous red circle with the yellow splat in the middle.

'Well, not just anybody,' said Ugenia with a bemused, puzzling smile.

Big News!

Hello, well aren't I all arty-farty or what?!

I don't know whether the Russian genius artist and the *Dona Plisa* thief are the same person. What do you think? Maybe it is the thief and he decided to STEAL an idea from a real artist – me!

Whatever Mr Poplin says, I still think anyone can paint if they put their mind to it, wherever they get their inspiration from.

Anyway, Uncle Harry and I had a great time together. He finally relaxed a bit . . . I reckon it was the glass licking that did it! There's a real art to being a professional glass licker. I don't recommend you try it unless you're stuck in a room and really thirsty!

And my parents really went to town on painting my bedroom. So things are looking up here in beige Boxmore . . . it's growing on me.

Extraordinary things can

happen even in ordinary places.
Cool, eh?!

Anyway, I gotta run . . . I'm
gonna paint the town red – joke!

Big XO
Ugenia Lavender XX

Ingenious Top Tip

Perfection kills art - let go and be a glass licker instead!

When I try to be perfect it spoils everything. I get so uptight I can't enjoy what I'm doing. It's a bit like Uncle Harry – he was so stressed about his spaghetti tomato sauce, he couldn't see how good it was until he loosened up and licked that glass.

Brain
Squeezers

Ugenia's Rucksack Riddle

My luminous yellow rucksack contains all the things I've found on my travels round the world. There's my stone from Nepal, a brown piece of rope from Iran, and five other things. Can you remember what they are? Fill in the spaces with the missing letters.

MAGNIFYING _Gl_ass

ELASTIC _band_

Nail VARNISH

BOTTLE _Top_

NOTE_Book_

Tip! If you're stuck, turn to pages 4 to 5 to refresh your memory.

Ugenia's Multi-Mix-Up!

Whoops! I've been writing a list of all the people in my life, but their names have got mixed up. Some of them are family, some are friends, and one person is not exactly a favourite of mine! Can you match the names up by drawing lines between them?

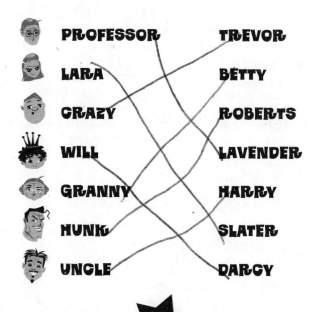

PROFESSOR	TREVOR
LARA	BETTY
CRAZY	ROBERTS
WILL	LAVENDER
GRANNY	HARRY
HUNK	SLATER
UNCLE	DARCY

Ugenia's Colour Crossword

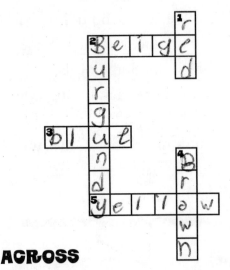

ACROSS

2. Our new house at 13 Cromer Road is this boring colour – on the outside, the inside and in my bedroom! Yawn!

3. Incredible! My parents then painted my bedroom this amazing bright colour (with a rainbow stripe too).

5. This is the lovely colour of my favourite luminous rucksack.

DOWN

1. Me and Uncle Harry foiled the *Dona Plisa* thief by splattering paint all over him. Can you remember what colour the paint was?

2. The colour of the sweaters that all the pupils wear at Boxmore Hill Junior School – my new school.

4. Remember the special things in my rucksack that I collected from around the world? This is the colour of the rope that I found in Iran.

Ugenia's Head-Scratching Quiz

Now you've read my book, see how much you know about my life!

1. What's the name of my favourite drink? *Tarberry*

2. Rudy, Bronte, Trevor and I organized a Valentine's Day Disco at school. What was the theme of the disco? *under the sea*

3. Who makes my heart beat like a drum and my legs feel like wibbly-wobbly jellies? *will Darcy*

4. Which country was I living in before I came to England? *Egypt*

5. What kind of creature is my dad, Professor Edward Lavender, an expert on? *Dinasoars*

Answers

Ugenia's Rucksack Riddle

MAGNIFYING GLASS

ELASTIC BAND

NAIL VARNISH

BOTTLE TOP

NOTEBOOK

Ugenia's Colour Crossword

ACROSS

2. BEIGE
3. BLUE
5. YELLOW

DOWN

1. RED
2. BURGUNDY
4. BROWN

Ugenia's Multi-Mix-up!

PROFESSOR – LAVENDER

LARA – SLATER

CRAZY – TREVOR

WILL – DARCY

GRANNY – BETTY

HUNK – ROBERTS

UNCLE – HARRY

Ugenia's Head-Scratching Quiz

1. Tarberry juice
2. Under-the-sea
3. Will Darcy
4. Egypt
5. Dinosaurs

Collect all 6
uGenia
Lavender
books!

Geri Halliwell

uGenia
Lavender

She's totally ingenious!

Got it! ☑

Geri Halliwell

uGenia
Lavender

and the Terrible Tiger

Got it! ☐

Geri Halliwell

uGenia
Lavender

and the Burning Pants

Got it! ☐

Got it! ☐

Got it! ☐

Got it! ☐

Collect all six books and get a FREE Ugenia Photo Frame!

UGeNIALaVeNder

Photo frame supplied without Geri's photo

There is a token in each Ugenia Lavender book – collect all six tokens and you can get your very own, totally free UGENIA LAVENDER photo frame!

Send your six tokens, along with your name, address and parent/guardian's signature (you must get your parent/guardian's signature to take part in this offer) to: Ugenia Lavender Photo Frame Offer, Marketing Dept, Macmillan Children's Books, The Macmillan Building, 4 Crinan Street, London N1 9XW

Ugenia Lavender Photo Frame Offer

Token 1

Collect all six tokens and get your free photo frame
Valid until 31/01/09

A selected list of titles available from Macmillan Children's Books

The prices shown below are correct at the time of going to press. However, Macmillan Publishers reserves the right to show new retail prices on covers, which may differ from those previously advertised.

All Pan Macmillan titles can be ordered from our website, www.panmacmillan.com, or from your local bookshop and are also available by post from:

Bookpost, PO Box 29, Douglas, Isle of Man IM99 1BQ
Credit cards accepted. For details:
Telephone: 01624 677237
Fax: 01624 670923
Email: bookshop@enterprise.net
www.bookpost.co.uk

Free postage and packing in the United Kingdom